A Marc Brown ARTHUR Chapter Book

Buster's
Dino Dilemma

Little, Brown and Company

Boston   New York   Toronto   London

3 1969 00999 2206

Copyright © 1998 by Marc Brown

First Edition

The characters and events portrayed in this book are fictitious. Any
similarity to real persons, living or dead, is coincidental and not intended
by the author.

Text by Stephen Krensky, based on the teleplay by Matt Steinglass
Text has been reviewed and assigned a reading level by Laurel S. Ernst,
M.A., Teachers College, Columbia University, New York, New York;
reading specialist, Chappaqua, New York

ISBN 0-316-11559-2 (hc)
ISBN 0-316-11560-6 (pb)
Library of Congress Catalog Card Number 98-65023

10 9 8 7 6 5 4 3 2 1

WOR (hc)
COM-MO (pb)

Published simultaneously in Canada by Little, Brown & Company
(Canada) Limited

Printed in the United States of America

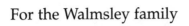
For the Walmsley family

Chapter 1

· · · · · · · · · · ·

"We're here!" Buster shouted.

The rest of Mr. Ratburn's third-grade class cheered.

They were riding in a school bus entering Rainbow Rock State Park. The class had come there for a field trip. The park was a great place to hunt for fossils of ancient animals — including dinosaurs.

As the bus pulled to a stop, Mr. Ratburn stood up.

"After we exit the bus," he said, "please line up outside in an orderly fashion."

The kids piled out quickly. The word *orderly* did not seem to be on anyone's mind.

Binky leapt out onto the pavement. He clawed at the air. "*T. rex*. Grrr!"

Francine lowered her head at him and stamped her foot. "Triceratops. Raarrr!"

Buster and Arthur stepped around these fierce beasts.

"I can't believe we're here!" said Buster.

"I can't believe you keep saying that," said Arthur.

"Well, I'm excited. I've been counting the hours, the minutes, the seconds. . . . I can't wait to get started."

Buster had become very interested in dinosaurs lately. He had read stacks of books from the library and had watched every dinosaur movie from the video store.

And today he had come specially prepared. Unlike the others, who were wearing their regular clothes, he had dressed very carefully.

"Isn't that hat hot?" Arthur asked.

Buster shook his head. "It's not a hat—it's a pith helmet. This is what paleontologists wear. It keeps them cool under the hot desert sun."

Arthur looked around. "Um, Buster, maybe you haven't noticed, but we're not in the desert."

Buster shrugged. "Well, I burn easily. And it's better to be ready for anything. Expect the unexpected, that's my motto." He patted his utility belt. "Which is why we brought along all these tools."

"Don't remind me," said Arthur, shifting his heavy backpack.

"You'll thank me later. We don't want to be caught unprepared. Hey, where did we put the chisels?"

"I've got them," said Arthur.

"What about the field guides?"

"Got those, too."

"Oooh! I hope we didn't forget—"

"Don't worry," said Arthur, patting his

side pocket. "I have the brushes right here."

Mr. Ratburn called for everyone's attention. "Excuse me, children. If you could please quiet down."

Some of the class turned toward him, but a few of the kids continued growling at one another.

"QUIET!" Mr. Ratburn shouted.

The growling stopped.

"Thank you," Mr. Ratburn said calmly. "As you know, we've come to the park today to learn more about dinosaurs and the evidence of their existence long ago."

He stared for a moment at Binky and Francine. "All dinosaurs and students need to be on their best behavior. Is that clear?"

Francine nodded. Binky just looked at the ground.

"Excellent," said Mr. Ratburn. "Now follow me, and we'll get started."

Chapter 2

• • • • • • • • • • • •

Mr. Ratburn led the way through the entrance into a small museum. In the first room there were some glass cases displaying bones and rocks. Along one wall was a diorama showing a brachiosaurus and a hadrosaurus eating in a swamp.

"I'd get tired of eating nothing but salad all day," said Francine.

Muffy agreed. "Even with the finest imported dressing, it would get pretty boring."

Mr. Ratburn had approached a park ranger who appeared to be waiting for him. They shook hands and exchanged hellos.

"Class, this is Ranger Ruth," Mr. Ratburn announced. "She's going to tell us a few things about fossils before we go out and explore for ourselves."

Ranger Ruth smiled sweetly at the class. "Hi, kids! Gosh, don't you look like a smart bunch of boys and girls! Can any of you tell me what a fossil is?"

A few kids rolled their eyes.

Buster raised his hand.

"Oh, good. A volunteer. Now, don't be shy. What do you think a fossil is?"

Buster took a deep breath. "Fossils are the calcified remains of ancient organisms. Minerals seep into these organisms' tissues and harden, preserving their original forms."

"Well, well, well!" Ranger Ruth looked stunned. "Count on me to pick out the class genius. Moving right along, we have a little show for you to see. LIGHTS!"

As the lights dimmed in the room, a spotlight shined on the dinosaur diorama.

Ranger Ruth spoke into a microphone. "A hundred million years ago, Rainbow Rock State Park looked very different. It was much hotter. There were lots of ferns."

At that moment, a park ranger dressed as a fern shuffled into view.

"There were also lots of insects," Ranger Ruth continued.

Another ranger, dressed as a dragonfly, flapped onto the stage.

"Ewwww!" said the class together.

"And, of course, there were dinosaurs." The kids cheered.

Two park rangers in a brachiosaurus costume stumbled onto the stage.

"Eventually, the ferns and animals died."

The fern costume slumped to the floor.

The kids giggled.

Then the dragonfly collapsed, and the brachiosaurus split apart, the front end remaining on the stage while the back end ran off.

Everyone laughed.

"Quiet, please!" said Mr. Ratburn.

"Thank you," said Ranger Ruth. "Now, usually the bodies would rot away. But once in a while, the hard parts of the bodies, like shells and bones, would last."

The front part of the brachiosaurus unzipped his costume, revealing a brachiosaurus skeleton costume underneath.

"Much much later, this whole area was covered by the sea. Over millions of years, the soil turned to rock. And the bones and shells turned to rock, too."

The light faded as the sound of crashing waves came over the loudspeakers.

"Then the sea dried up. And finally,

after another hundred million years, we're up to the present."

A spotlight was switched on, revealing a giant brachiosaurus skeleton on the far side of the hall.

The kids applauded as the lights came back on.

"Now," said Ranger Ruth, "who wants to go on a fossil hunt?"

Chapter 3

• • • • • • • • • • • •

The class hiked behind Ranger Ruth through a valley rimmed with high shale cliffs. Everyone was carrying a pail and shovel.

"I'm so excited!" Buster told Arthur.

"Really? I never would have guessed."

"I can't wait to get my hands on one of those fossils," Buster went on. "I mean, it's the real thing. The actual impression of something that was alive millions of years ago."

"Your attention, please!" said Ranger Ruth. "Listen up!"

The class had stopped in front of one

of the cliffs. The layers of dirt and rock made different-colored stripes in the cliff wall.

"You see the layers in this rock?" Ranger Ruth continued. "Each layer was formed at a different time. The ones on the bottom are from the beginning of the Cretaceous period, around 135 million years ago."

"Wow," said Binky, "that was even before TV."

"Now, the top layers are from about twenty million years later," the ranger continued. "So we can tell how old a fossil is by noting where it was found in the cliff."

Muffy looked confused. "How will we get fossils out of the cliff?" she asked. "All we have are these little buckets."

"Don't worry," said Ranger Ruth. "The cliffs are for the professional paleontologists. You kids will hunt in the stream."

"In the stream?" said Francine. "Great!"

She rushed into the water and began splashing around.

"The water's great," she shouted. "Hey, look, I found a fossil! Oh, no, wait. It's a rock. Hey, here's another one!"

All of the children soon followed in after her.

Mr. Ratburn walked around, giving words of encouragement. When he reached Arthur and Buster, he stopped to watch. Buster was bobbing up and down, frantically searching for fossils.

"Found anything yet, boys?"

"Noooooo!" they answered together.

"Oh. Well, we're going to break for a snack now, and then we'll be heading back to the bus."

Arthur straightened up. "Well," he said, stretching, "I guess that's that."

"I'm not stopping till the very last minute," said Buster.

Arthur looked over at Mr. Ratburn and the ranger. They were getting out juice and cookies from an ice chest.

"Buster! I see food! And drink!"

"I don't care," said Buster. "We can have snacks anytime. There are fossils here!"

"Are you sure you're feeling okay, Buster? I've never seen you turn down food before."

"Yes, I'm okay. I'm more than okay."

"Come on, then," said Arthur. "What do you expect to find in just a few more minutes? You're not going to just reach in and find something!"

Arthur reached his hand underwater and pulled up a stone with some markings on it.

Buster turned to him angrily. Then his expression went blank when he saw what Arthur had in his hand.

"Buster? Are you okay?"

Buster began advancing slowly toward him. His hands were outstretched.

Arthur backed away. "Buster? Quit it! You're making me nervous."

Arthur dropped the stone.

"Aaaaahhhhh!" said Buster.

He dove at the spot where the special stone fell in and began picking up any stone he could find. He glanced at each one, then threw it away.

"Buster, have you gone nuts?"

Buster picked up another stone, almost threw it away, too, and then clutched it to his chest.

"I found it! I found it!"

Arthur came over to see. "Found what?" he asked. "Show me."

Buster did. The stone showed an imprint with a three-pronged indentation.

"Oh, wow," said Arthur. "It's a leaf fossil."

"A leaf fossil? What do you mean, a leaf

fossil? Have you even seen a leaf that thick?"

Buster held it up to the light. He took a deep breath. "Arthur," he declared, "*this* is a footprint."

Chapter 4

• • • • • • • • • • •

As the other kids ate their snacks, Buster sat with one hand clenched on his pocket.

"Do you want a cookie, Buster?" Arthur asked.

Buster shook his head.

"How about some juice?"

Buster shook his head again. He was too excited to eat or drink. He was having enough trouble just breathing. Imagine! He had found a real dinosaur fossil. He could see the newspaper headlines now: BUSTER BAXTER'S BIG BREAK. Paleontologists from around the world would line up just to shake his hand.

Ranger Ruth brushed a few cookie crumbs off her shirt. "I think everyone worked up quite an appetite," she said. "While you finish up, let's go around and talk about the fossils we found."

Alex and the Brain held up a gray rock with grooves spreading from the center.

"We think this might have been a shell," said the Brain.

Ranger Ruth took the rock and examined it. "Very nice. And not just any shell. It looks like Emarginula."

She placed it in a box.

Alex and the Brain looked pleased. "Do you think it will end up on display?" the Brain asked.

"We'll see," said the ranger. "A lot of people beside myself are part of that decision."

Buster blinked. "Wait a minute!" he cried. "Can't we all keep what we found?"

Ranger Ruth shook her head. "Oh, I'm

sorry. Maybe you weren't listening when I explained earlier. We put as many fossils as we can in the museum so everyone can have a chance to see them."

"And you include proper credit," said the Brain.

"Absolutely," said the ranger. "We always give credit to whoever finds our fossils."

She smiled at Buster. "Okay?"

"I guess." Buster sat down again. "I can't believe it," he muttered to himself. "How can they do this to me?"

Francine held up some rocks. "Take a look at these. I don't think there are any fossils here. But the rocks are still pretty interesting."

The ranger examined them. "Yes, they are. Streaks of mica and quartz, I believe. I think I'll hold on to them for further study."

Francine beamed. "See that," she said to

Muffy. "Further study. I found important rocks."

Muffy shrugged. "The only really important rocks are the kind in rings and necklaces."

"Anyone else?" said Ranger Ruth.

A few more kids showed her what they had found.

Arthur poked Buster in the side.

"Stop that!" whispered Buster.

"But . . . but . . . ," began Arthur.

"Do you boys have something to add?" the ranger asked. "Did our budding expert find anything he'd like to share?"

"Nothing," said Buster. "Nothing at all."

Arthur looked surprised. "What do you mean?" he whispered. "I thought we—"

Buster elbowed Arthur in the ribs. "It's okay," he told Ranger Ruth. "Arthur's a little embarrassed because we don't have anything to show you."

The ranger patted Arthur on the back. "Don't worry about it, Arthur. As scientists, we must learn patience. I'm sure you'll find something another time."

"I guess so," said Arthur, glancing darkly at Buster. "I feel better already."

Chapter 5

• • • • • • • • • • •

There was still a little time for the kids to play before they had to leave. Binky went back to being a *T. rex*, growling and clawing at everyone who passed by. Francine and Muffy swooped over the grass as pterodactyls looking for something to eat.

Arthur wasn't in the mood to play dinosaur. He was nervous.

"We're never going to get away with this," he told Buster quietly as they sat at a picnic table.

"We'll see," said Buster.

"But the fossil isn't ours — I mean,

yours. I mean, you should get credit for finding it, but it belongs in the museum."

"I'm not giving it up," said Buster. He squeezed the fossil gently. "It's like holding a piece of history."

"But what if they search us on the way out? We could get arrested! What if they have some special fossil-detector alarm?"

"I've never heard of such a thing."

"Well, that doesn't make me feel better," said Arthur. "Remember, the time Muffy brought goat cheese to class and you insisted it was fake—because you had never heard of it?"

"That was different," said Buster. "It doesn't make sense that goats can make cheese if all they eat are tin cans."

"Well, you found out differently, didn't you? And what about that *Bionic Bunny* episode where the scientist invents an

X-ray laser? They could have one of those here."

Arthur looked around nervously.

"But *The Bionic Bunny* is a TV show," said Buster.

"I know. A lot of it is very realistic, though. Based on true stories, I think."

"Maybe so," said Buster, "but I don't think—"

Tweeeeeeet!

Mr. Ratburn was blowing his whistle.

"All right, everyone," he shouted, "let's gather round. The bus is here. Check your belongings to make sure you don't leave anything behind."

Buster put his hand back on his pocket. The fossil was safe. His finger could feel the rough outline of the footprint.

"Uh-oh," said Arthur. "Look, Buster, Ranger Ruth is coming toward us. She's going to frisk us. I told you this would happen. But did you want to listen? Noooooo. They must have some kind of detector hidden in the trees. It's probably triggered by an infrared—"

"Sssssh!" hissed Buster.

Ranger Ruth came right up to Buster and stopped.

"Any last thing you want to ask me?" she said.

"Um, I don't think so."

The ranger laughed. "Well, perhaps there's something you want to tell me instead."

"What kind of thing?"

"Well, I'm not sure. It could be some new dinosaur fact. Or maybe . . ."

Arthur squeezed his eyes shut. It was coming. The gamma-ray detection net had caught them for sure. They were goners.

". . . you might want to tell me you had a good time."

Buster brightened at once. "Oh, yes."

"You look a little uncomfortable," said the ranger. She patted Buster on the back. "I hope you're not too discouraged about your fossil hunting. You have the makings of a real paleontologist."

"Thanks."

She went off to say good-bye to Mr. Ratburn.

"See?" said Buster. "We're perfectly safe."

"Maybe for now," said Arthur.

Chapter 6

● ● ● ● ● ● ● ● ● ● ●

After school, Arthur wanted to tell Francine and the Brain about the fossil, but Buster wouldn't allow it.

"Too dangerous," he explained.

"Well, who *can* we tell?" Arthur asked.

"Nobody. We have to keep it a secret."

When Buster got home, he went straight to his room. He closed the door and pulled down his window shade.

"Perimeter security in place," he said.

Next, he wrapped the fossil in tinfoil. Then he put it inside a plastic bag and put the bag in a shoe box.

"Phase One complete."

He filled the rest of the shoe box with marbles from a bowl and put it on a shelf in his closet.

"Phase Two complete," he said. "Security protocol set. Alert status confirmed."

At dinner with his mother and grandmother, Buster didn't say much.

"Are you feeling okay?" his mother asked. "You're awfully quiet."

"Just tired, I guess," said Buster.

"How did the field trip go?"

"Okay," said Buster.

"Did you find any nice fossils?"

Buster almost knocked over his milk.

"Fossils? What makes you ask that?"

"I don't know, Buster. I thought that's why you went to the park."

"Oh, right. Well, it was pretty interesting. There was a show. The ranger was friendly. And then we got to walk around."

His mother nodded. "I'm glad you enjoyed yourself."

"When I was your age," said Buster's grandmother, "we didn't go fossil hunting." She paused. "Back then, dinosaurs were still alive, of course."

Buster's mother laughed.

Buster just rolled his eyes.

"What's that you've done to your mashed potatoes?" his mother asked.

Buster looked down at his plate.

"It kind of looks like a dinosaur footprint," his mother went on.

"No, no," said Buster, scooping up a bite and swallowing it. "Just a design. That's all."

A little later, Buster went up to his room for the night. He tossed and turned a long time before he finally fell asleep.

Thummmp! Thummp!

"What's that noise?" Buster wondered. He looked out his window.

A large dinosaur was looking back at him.

"There you are!" said the dinosaur.

"Who, me?" said Buster.

"Yes, you—the boy who took my footprint. I want it back—now!"

"I think you're confusing me with somebody else," said Buster.

"No, I'm not," said the dinosaur. "Maybe you think you can ignore me because I'm not that big. Don't be fooled. I have big and powerful friends."

The dinosaur flicked his tail behind him. Buster saw a tyrannosaurus and a triceratops standing there. The tyrannosaurus, though, had Binky's head, and the triceratops had Francine's.

"Give back the footprint!" they shouted.

"Never!" said Buster, and he slammed the window shut.

What was he going to do? What were they going to do?

Suddenly the room began to shake. His

books tumbled off their shelves, and a box of colored pencils spilled onto the floor.

"We're coming!" said the voices outside. "We want the footprint!"

Buster grabbed the shoe box with the fossil in it and held it tightly.

The room trembled around him, and he waited for the end to come.

Chapter 7

• • • • • • • • • • • •

"Wow!" said Arthur. "That was some dream."

He and Buster were sitting at their desks before class started the next morning. Buster had been relating the details of his nightmare.

"The worst part," said Buster, "was that Binky's head looked so natural on top of the tyrannosaurus."

"What about Francine's?"

Buster laughed. He looked at Francine, who was talking with Muffy and Sue Ellen on the other side of the room. "She never looks completely normal," he said.

Arthur nodded. He was happy Buster had told him about the dream, but he was even happier he hadn't dreamed it himself.

"At least it's over," said Buster.

"True," said Arthur. "But don't you think your dream was trying to tell you something?"

Buster considered it.

"Yes, it was telling me not to put so much chocolate sauce on my apple pie. I think I got a little stomachache before bedtime."

Arthur sighed. "So when can I come over and see it?"

"You can't. No one can."

Arthur looked surprised. "Why not?"

"I've made very careful security arrangements. They should not be disturbed."

"I'll be careful," Arthur insisted.

"Sorry. It's too dangerous. What if my mom came in?"

"But Buster, what's the point of having the you-know-what if we can't even look at it?"

Buster was saved from trying to answer that question because Francine was on her way over.

"Good morning, Arthur. You look kind of tired, Buster. Didn't sleep well, huh? Probably feeling bad because you didn't find anything yesterday."

"What do you mean?"

"I mean at the park. You're the big expert, Mr. Paleontologist."

Buster's face got red. "It's true that I like fossils."

"And yet with all your knowledge, all your tools . . . and, yes, let's not forget your hat—"

"Pith helmet," Buster corrected her.

"Pith helmet," Francine repeated. "Even with all that, you didn't find anything."

Buster was silent.

"You're not being fair, Francine," said Arthur. "Buster did a good job looking yesterday." Arthur stared hard at Francine. "A really good job."

She just laughed.

"Excuse me," said Mr. Ratburn. "Let's take our places."

When the whole class was seated, he continued.

"I hope you all enjoyed our field trip yesterday. I know it was exciting to have the chance to find a real fossil. Of course, finding them isn't easy. It would have been amazing if we had found signs of any dinosaur bones or teeth."

Arthur fidgeted a little while Buster put his hands over his mouth and covered his eyes with his long ears.

"Or, even rarer, dinosaur footprints. Wouldn't that have been exciting?"

Everyone nodded.

Mr. Ratburn shrugged. "But this time it didn't happen. What's that, Buster?"

"Nothing, Mr. Ratburn."

"Oh. I thought I heard you groan. Well, anyway, just remember that throughout history the great scientists have met with disappointment first and then triumphed later on."

Buster slumped forward on his desk. Keeping this secret was getting to be a lot harder than he had thought.

Chapter 8

• • • • • • • • • • • •

Mrs. Baxter was worried.

"Are you okay, honey?" she asked.

Buster jumped off his bed. "Okay? Of course, I'm okay. Why wouldn't I be okay? Don't I look okay?"

His mother wasn't so sure. "Well, you look a little tired. You're not having any problems at school, are you?"

"No, no," said Buster, "everything at school is fine."

The phone rang.

Buster ran to answer it.

"Hello?"

"Hi," said Arthur. "I had a question about our math homework. Are we supposed to measure things by the *foot* or the *meter?*"

"*Foot?* What makes you say *foot?*"

"How else should I say it?" Arthur asked.

"You don't fool me," said Buster. "You know perfectly well we're supposed to do both. You're just checking up on my *you-know-what.*"

"Honestly, Buster, I couldn't remember if —"

"Yeah, yeah. Nice try, Arthur. I'll see you tomorrow. Bye."

He hung up the phone and returned to his room.

He found his mother holding the shoe box.

"What's this, Buster? It feels kind of heavy."

"That?" Buster rushed over and took it

out of her hand. "It's a school project. Very delicate. Hush-hush. Top secret. Can't talk about it now."

He put it back in the closet.

His mother looked concerned. "You need some rest, honey. Maybe you should go to bed early."

Buster glanced at the window. "Bed? Early?" he squeaked. "Sounds good."

Sometime later, Buster lay in bed, thinking about fossils. His eyelids began to droop.

There was a knock at the door.

"Who is it?" asked Buster.

"Fossil Police."

"Huh?" said Buster.

The door burst open. Ranger Ruth and a police officer entered. They were dragging Arthur behind them. He was wearing a striped prisoner's uniform.

"I'm sorry, Buster," said Arthur. "They made me tell. They tickled me."

"Why didn't you defend yourself?" Buster asked.

Arthur held up his arms. He was wearing handcuffs.

"Not a pretty picture, is it?" said Ranger Ruth. "And we've got the same treatment ready for you."

"Me?" said Buster. "What did I do?"

The ranger laughed. "We have reason to believe you're hiding a dinosaur in this room."

Buster's eyes darted to his closet. "But that's ridiculous! There haven't been any dinosaurs for millions of years. How could—"

Ranger Ruth and the officer followed Buster's gaze to his closet. Then they halted, hearing a strange sound.

Tromp, tromp, tromp.

"Care to explain that, Mr. Paleontologist?" asked Ranger Ruth.

"Explain what?" said Buster. "I don't hear anything."

TROMP, TROMP, TROMP.

"Stand back," said the ranger. "We're about to—"

Suddenly the closet door burst open. A Tyrannosaurus rex stepped out, roaring at them.

"Guilty as charged," said the ranger.

"He looks hungry," said Arthur.

"Don't worry," said the ranger. "We're perfectly safe. He's only mad at Buster for keeping him cooped up in the closet."

The tyrannosaurus opened his mouth wide, showing every one of his teeth.

Buster screamed.

Chapter 9

• • • • • • • • • • • •

Buster was absent from school the next day. Arthur wasn't really worried because he figured that Buster was just sick. But he decided to go by the Baxters' apartment on his way home.

Mrs. Baxter let him in.

"Hello, Arthur, how are you?"

"Fine."

Mrs. Baxter sighed. "I wish I could say the same for Buster. I kept him home today because he didn't sleep well last night. I don't think he's sick or contagious, though, so you can go see him."

"Thanks, Mrs. Baxter."

When Arthur reached Buster's room, he found the door closed. He knocked.

"Buster! It's me, Arthur."

Buster opened the door. He was still wearing his pajamas.

"You're just in time, Arthur. I need help with the final preparations."

Arthur blinked. The room was a mess. Everything had been emptied out of the closet, and there was a web of string criss-crossing the room.

"What are you doing?" Arthur asked.

"Well, first I emptied my closet. That way I can tell what's inside with a quick look. I don't want any dinosaurs hiding in there." He pointed to the string. "And now I'm making a dinosaur detector. When the dinosaurs come, they're not going to catch me by surprise."

"But Buster, dinosaurs have been extinct for millions of years. You know that."

"I think that's just what they want us to believe. It's all part of their master plan."

"Their master plan?"

Buster nodded. "That's why they've left all those fossils to find. They want to trick us. But I'm not fooled. I'm going to be ready."

Arthur sat down on the bed.

"Don't you think you're going a little overboard?"

Buster snorted. "You wouldn't say that if you'd had the dream I had last night. Actually, you were there. Not the real you, of course, but the dream you. It was pretty scary."

He took out a shoe box from under the bed.

"Here," said Buster. "You take this."

"Why?"

"The fossil's inside. You said you wanted to see it before. Now you can have it."

"Buster, I don't want the fossil, either. It isn't right."

Buster rubbed his eyes. "I have to get rid of it, Arthur. I'm going crazy."

Arthur took another look around the room. "So I see," he said.

"I thought it would be so great, having this million-year-old thing to myself. I thought I would feel special and important. But all I feel is . . ."

"Guilty?"

Buster paced back and forth. "I don't know. But it's driving me nuts, that's for sure. I can't even look at it anymore."

Arthur stared at the box. "The fossil doesn't belong here or at my house," he said. "You know that."

Buster sighed. "So where *does* it belong?"

Arthur gave him a look. "*You* tell *me*," he said.

Chapter 10

• • • • • • • • • • • • •

Inside the Rainbow Rock Visitor Center, Arthur and Buster were anxiously standing by the door.

"They're taking a long time," said Buster. He rubbed his hands together. "Maybe we shouldn't have come."

Arthur tried to smile. "Now, don't start *that* again. . . ."

Buster paced back and forth. "I can't help it," he said. "I'm not good at waiting. Do you think there's a problem?"

"I sure hope not," said Arthur.

Finally, Ranger Ruth approached them.

One of the staff paleontologists was with her.

"Good afternoon, boys," she said. "I'm glad to see you again."

"And we're glad to be here," said Arthur. He looked nervously at Buster. "Aren't we?"

Buster nodded. "So, what can you tell us?" he asked excitedly.

Ranger Ruth folded her arms. "No decision has been made."

Arthur sighed.

"Basically, we're just not sure yet," said the paleontologist.

"Still?" said Buster. It had been a whole month since he and Arthur had returned the fossil to Ranger Ruth. They had surprised her, both because the fossil was rare and because Buster had taken it from the park in the first place. But she was pleased that he had returned it. And when she heard about his nightmares, she decided to go easy on him.

The paleontologist smiled. "I understand how you feel, Buster. Unfortunately, these things take time. We have to do a spectral analysis, carbon-14 dating . . ."

"I know, I know," said Buster. "Science can't be rushed. But I was hoping for a decision before *I* become a fossil."

"We're getting closer," said the paleontologist. "Dr. Marsh thinks your fossil is the footprint of a baby daspletosaurus. Dr. Cope, however, thinks it's an adult coelosaur."

"And what do you think?" asked Arthur.

"I think it's great that you two found the fossil in the first place."

Buster beamed. "It did take a lot of looking." He stopped to think. "The odds were against us. Luckily, we had brought our tools. The pith helmet especially helped a

lot. I could see the fossil clearly when Arthur held it up. I might have missed it otherwise."

"Speaking of not missing things," said Ranger Ruth, "I want to show you something."

She walked them over to the display case.

Next to the fossil footprint was a brass plaque. It read *Dinosaur Footprint, Discovered by Buster Baxter and Arthur Read.*

"Wow!" said Buster. "Our very own nameplate."

"I've never seen my name look so fancy," said Arthur.

"I think it's gold," said Buster. He paused. "But how long does it get to stay there?"

"For as long as the fossil lasts," said Ranger Ruth.

Buster smiled. "That's long enough for me," he said.